Father Félix

The Shepherdess of Lourdes

Or, the blind princess. A drama in five acts.

Father Félix

The Shepherdess of Lourdes
Or, the blind princess. A drama in five acts.

ISBN/EAN: 9783337394646

Printed in Europe, USA, Canada, Australia, Japan

Cover: Foto ©Andreas Hilbeck / pixelio.de

More available books at **www.hansebooks.com**

THE
SHEPHERDESS
OF LOURDES

OR

THE BLIND PRINCESS ·

A DRAMA IN FIVE ACTS

BY

V. REV. F. FELIX, O.S.B., D.D.
Author of "Walburga," "Pontia," "Patricia."

FIFTH EDITION

JOHN MURPHY COMPANY
PUBLISHERS

200 W. LOMBARD STREET   BALTIMORE, MD.

PREFACE

The famous shrine of Our Lady of Lourdes continues to attract the attention of the Christian World. Thousands of Catholics and non Catholics visit annually the sacred Grotto; and extraordinary cures, effected by the use of the miraculous water, are of daily occurrence. The faithful have, in both hemispheres, erected Grottoes similar to the grand original in France, in veneration of the Virgin Immaculate, who there deigned to manifest herself to the poor shepherdess, Bernadette Soubirons, in 1858. A drama, therefore, representing the first days of that wonderful sanctuary, cannot fail to interest and please. I have been faithful to history as far as circumstances permitted. Though I confess that Rosabella, the blind Princess, whose cure is so realistically presented, is not an historic character, yet many similar miracles have been authenticated, so that truth will not suffer. For the leading idea in the play I am indebted to Dr. Robert Weissenhofer who, in German, published a similar one, which was gratefully received by the public in Europe.

I dedicate this drama to the Immaculate Mother, and to a little band of her children in North Carolina —.the pupils of the Sacred Heart Academy, at Belmont.

THE AUTHOR.

CAST OF CHARACTERS

BERNADETTE, the Shepherdess.

LOUISA, Her Mother.

ELENORA, Princess of Valencia.

ROSABELLA, Her Blind Daughter.

LUCILLA, Her Younger Daughter.

LAURINDA, a Governess.

ANTONIA,
MINA, } Ladies of the Palace.

GERTRUDE, Castle Keeper's Wife.

AGNES,
STELLA, } Her Daughters.
TERESA,

MME. MASSAY, the Governor's Wife.

MME. DOZONS, the Physician's Wife.

MLLE. VERGEZ, Niece of Mme. Massay.

ISABELLA, Gertrude's Friend.

LYDIA, Gypsy Girl.

MARIE, Bernadette's Younger Sister.

JOSEPHA,
AMALIA, } Children of Lourdes.
INEZ,
HELEN,

Eight Angels, one Guardian Angel, Girls and Ladies from Lourdes.

STAGE DIRECTIONS

A grotto or cave can easily be erected in the rear of any stage by using dark or gray canvas. The Virgin in Acts I and III may be represented by a young lady dressed as the Madonna of Lourdes. A statue of the Blessed Virgin is necessary for Act V; however, any statue of the Holy Mother would answer the purpose. Rosabella is supposed to be fourteen years old — the age of Bernadette. Simplicity in action is required. As a blind girl she may wear dark glasses, which she leaves in the cave whilst apparently bathing her eyes in Act III. No institute should find difficulties to render this drama with but medium talent.

THE SHEPHERDESS OF LOURDES

ACT I

SCENE.—*Garden or forest scene.—Background repre-*
sents the Grotto of Lourdes.—In the rocks a large
cave.

[*Eight little* ANGELS *kneel, facing the empty cave.*
Music plays solemnly as the curtain is lifted.

Red Light. When BERNADETTE *begins to speak, the*
ANGELS *slowly withdraw behind the wings on*
both sides of the stage.]

Bernadette [*behind the scenes, slowly*]. Only the
small path, and we have reached the spot. Be brave,
mother, and follow me. Here it is dangerous; so, be
careful now.

Louisa. Take good care of yourself, daughter; I
am safe.

Enter BERNADETTE *and* LOUISA.

Bernadette. Here we are at last, good mother, in
the holy, heaven-blessed abode of spirits. Oh, mother!
do you feel the happiness, the joy of this place; can you
breathe the celestial odor? I always imagine that a
choir of angels must here have their dwelling.

Louisa. Is this the cave, daughter; and here you saw
the vision?

Bernadette. Yes; there, there, mother—from within
those rocks she comes. Oh, could you only see her!

5

Louisa. Strange! I never knew such a place was near our home. See the rough rocks, the ivy and moss-covered cave; yonder the peaceful Gave streaming along its usual course — beautiful, mysterious. How does the lady look who appeared to you, daughter?

Bernadette. Oh, she was heavenly fair! Mother, I cannot describe her beauty; in my life I have never seen anything half as beautiful as she was.

Louisa. Oh, you dreamed, Bernadette, you dreamed!

Bernadette. Dreamed! Never! My two eyes are witness to what I have seen; my whole self, trans-formed in sweet ecstasy, has felt this heavenly being. Marie, my sister, was with me and Jeane—we gathered wood here in this place—when suddenly this vision came upon me.

Louisa. But neither of them have seen anything.

Bernadette. They saw nothing. Oh, that I alone should have been so favored! Yet they were not with me then, dear mother; I was here alone. We had to cross the water to reach yonder banks, and I sat down here to take off my shoes; when suddenly I heard the rushing wind. Then the Angelus bell rang in our little village church. I knelt down to say my *Ave,* and had scarcely begun: "Hail, full of grace," when, lo!— mother, can you believe it?—a woman of incomparable splendor stood upright within the cave, in the midst of an unearthly brightness. Oh, mother, believe me! she was no mere phantom; but life and reality. She was quite young, and had features of superhuman beauty. Never have I seen such beautiful eyes, or such a fair countenance. Her garments, mother, must have been woven in heaven; they were purer than the lilies of the valley, and as white as the stainless mountain snow. Her robe was long, and on her bare feet rested two golden roses. In front, a girdle — blue as heaven, mother — falling in two long bands nearly to her feet. A white veil was fixed around her head, and fell in ample folds to her shoulders. She wore neither ring, necklace, nor crown; but on her arm hung a chaplet, with beads as white as drops of milk, strung on a golden chain. Her hands were fervently clasped, as if in prayer. All this I saw, mother; yet no one could describe her beauty.

Louisa. And what did you do, child?

Bernadette. I took my little rosary in my hands, and prayed loud and fervently: "Hail, Mary, full of grace." And when I had finished the decades, the white lady disappeared. I heard nothing then but the murmurs of the Gave passing over the rocks and pebbles. I had been in heaven, mother, and now I was on earth once more. These poor rocks looked then so sadly upon me, and I wept. I called Marie and Jeane — they were gone; they thought I was praying.

Louisa. And who do you think the lady was?

Bernadette. Mother, do not ask me this question; you might think me presumptuous.

Louisa. But I demand an answer.

Bernadette [*with downcast eyes and trembling*]. Our Blessed Lady.

Louisa. Truly you are presumptuous, girl. How can you, a poor shepherdess, expect such a favor. Surely you were deceived, daughter; such thoughts should not enter your mind. I am ashamed of you.

Bernadette [*confused*]. Forgive me, mother, for saying so; but could you feel my little heart — how it beats! It may have been my guardian angel. And yesterday, mother, I stole away from home and came here—I had some holy water with me. I prayed; and again the white lady appeared. I said: "If you come on the part of God, approach"; and threw holy water at the vision. I could say no more, mother; and imagine, the apparition smiled a heavenly smile, mother —such as angels smile. She looked upon me so kindly, so gently, that great big tears ran down my cheeks. I felt so ashamed of myself, so little, mother.

Louisa. That will do. You must drive these thoughts from you; you are becoming a dreamer. I will send you to your aunt on the mountains. Work will soon change your mind.

Bernadette. Whenever you wish to send me, I am willing to go, mother; but I cannot believe that I was dreaming, nor that I saw nothing uncommon, for either would be deception. Oh, would that one ray of that heavenly light, which appeared to me here, could be visible to you — you would believe me.

Louisa. Be it as it may. It is nearly sunset; so let us return home. Come!

Bernadette. Mother — I cannot call you anything sweeter than this lovely name, "mother"—grant your daughter one request.

Louisa. Speak, daughter.

Bernadette. Let me remain here, only for a little while longer. Oh, mother! if you could feel as I do;

if you could look into my very soul, and perceive that yearning and that desire to remain, feel that happiness which I experience—that inexpressible joy! [*Falls on her knees.*] In the name of the Blessed Mother, who deigned to appear to your unworthy daughter, let me remain here.

Louisa. You are bold in making such a request. Arise! and do not speak in such terms of your supposed vision.

Bernadette. They are not my words; something in me speaks to you. Let me remain, I beseech you.

Louisa. Well—remain, then.

[BERNADETTE *arises and falls on her neck.*]

Bernadette. A thousand thanks, mother, dear; a thousand thanks. May heaven reward you. I shall be home shortly after the Angelus tolls. Now let me help you to descend these rocky paths.

Louisa [*looks around once more*]. Poor deceived creature, something must have charmed you. Well, we will see. [*They depart,* BERNADETTE *leading her mother.*]

VILLAGE CHILDREN *enter from opposite side of the stage. One carries a bundle of rough wood; others, small baskets.*

Marie. Come, come, girls, here is an open place. Come, girls, here we can play.

Josepha. How lovely it is here; see the rocks!

Marie [*in astonishment*]. Oh, girls! this is the place where sister saw the white ghost a few days ago.

All. Ghost! a ghost!

Marie. Yes, surely; sitting on the rocks, over there.

Inez. You frighten us.

All. Let us go! Marie, please let us go.

Marie. No, stay, stay; the ghost was a good one, and would hurt no one. Let us sit down.

Helen. No, let us play something, Marie.

All. What?

Josepha. "Hide and seek," or anything else. Let us dance.

Marie. But don't come near yonder rocks.

> [*She walks up to the cave. They give a short dance. Music.* MARIE *returning, and speaking slow and solemn.*]

No, no! do not dance here, girls. Pray do not dance here.

All [*stopping*]. Why not?

Marie. I don't know; but something—[*Looks shyly about.*]

All. What's the matter?

Marie. It's all over now. Come, let us sit down.

> [*All sit around* MARIE.]

I think my sister Bernadette will soon come; I heard her voice down near the saw-mill. She will tell us all she has seen here.

Amalia. Don't frighten us so.

Ines. Perhaps some one was killed here long ago, that a poor soul comes back asking for prayers; they often do.

Josepha. Yes, yes, you remember·poor Eliza's boy, who drowned in the miller's pond; he came back, they say.

Helen. My mother swears that she hears someone knocking on our back door every midnight.

Amalia. I am afraid ever since my grandfather died. You can never make me go into that room alone.

Marie. Foolish girls, there are no ghosts here; so that's all. Now stop your foolish talk, and sing with me a hymn; in this way we can spend the time best, and arrange our flowers and ferns.

[*They sing.*]

As the dewy shades of even'
   Gather o'er the balmy air,
Listen, gentle Queen of Heaven,
   Listen to our evening prayer.
Holy Mother, near us hover,
   Free our thoughts from aught defiled;
With thy wings of mercy cover,
   Safe from harm, thy helpless child.

Towards the end, BERNADETTE *enters. She claps her hands.* CHILDREN *arise, surround* BERNADETTE *and say:*

All. Bernadette! Oh, Bernadette!

Bernadette. Good, good, children; you could not have found a sweeter place than this for such a lovely

song. Your angels must rejoice, listening to your
prayers. Marie, mother is waiting for you near the
mill; she is speaking to Jeane, who wants to see you.

Marie. Will you not return with us; it is growing
late.

Bernadette. No, girls—Oh! what shall I tell them?
no, girls, I wish to remain here, all alone. I love this
spot, and that cave; I wish to say my rosary. You will
be good children, and leave me alone, will you not?

Josepha. Let us say the rosary with you.

Bernadette [*confused*]. Not now girls, dear, your
mothers would look for you; it is late, and I would
receive the blame for detaining you. You would not
wish me to be blamed, would you?

All. No, Bernadette, you are always so good.

Bernadette. Well, then, go home, and say your
rosary at home; and tomorrow you can all come to
our garden, and I will give each one a bunch of strawberries.

All. Strawberries! That's nice!

Ines. Come, children, let us leave Bernadette and
return home.

All. Let us go home.

> [*They take their little baskets;* AMALIA, *a bundle
> of wood.*]

Bernadette. See, see how diligent Amalia was; she
has gathered a big bundle of wood.

All. But we helped her!

Bernadette. That's good! Now help her carry it
home.

Marie. Come home soon, sister.

Bernadette. Good-bye, girls.

All. Good-bye; we will see you tomorrow.

[*They leave the stage very noisily; talking, and at times screaming: "Look out," etc., till they are far off.*]

Bernadette [*watching the children departing*]. Poor children, there is nothing extraordinary to them in this spot. Here they play and sing, here they tell their little stories. And to me every stone is sacred; the very soil upon which I tread, consecrated. I brought my mother here, today, at her own request—I permit no secret between her and myself. But she disbelieves me, she mocks me, she threatens to send me back to the Pyrenees to watch the cattle; for which I am better suited, she says. Maybe. But David was a shepherd boy, and he became the ruler of his nation. Mary, a poor virgin of Galilee, was called to be God's mother. Joan of Arc, as a shepherdess, heard supernatural voices; and she delivered our country and king, and crowned him at Rheims. But why such thoughts? Pride, wicked pride has prompted these. Bernadette, beware of deceit, fear sin, and remain the humble maiden of the Pyrenees. I was happy when, on the everlasting hills, I sought pasture for my sheep—they were my sole companions; shared my sorrow and my joy—and with the birds I sang and played. I was happy then. To God I gave my heart in prayer; and with the rising and the setting sun I greeted Him, begging Him to protect His lonely child. These days are gone. I am now a dreamer, a visionary; possibly, a young witch. People point their fingers at me, and call me mad. My father's hut will soon be closed to me, if I persist in telling the truth. May God help poor Bernadette, the shepherdess of Lourdes. The sun is bidding the day farewell. Soon the harmonious sounds of the Angelus bell will vibrate through this peaceful valley. The day is done; how I tremble. Poor little heart! Why this fright, Bernadette? Can it be possible; will she come again? [*Turns to the grotto.*] Oh, blessed grotto! happy abode of unknown spirits, the mystical dove has left the heavenly abode, she dwelt here—rested her virgin feet upon the ivy-clad rocks, nestled in the mystic crevice. Come, my fair one, my love, my dove!

[*The Angelus bell rings at Lourdes. A brilliant light fills the entire grotto.* BERNADETTE *falls on her knees and says, loud and distinctly:*]

Hail—Mary—full—of—grace—the—Lord—is—with—thee.

[*Music plays softly. The* "White Lady" *appears.*

CURTAIN.

ACT II

SCENE.—*In the castle of the Prince of Valencia, at San Sebastiano, Spain. A luxuriously furnished apartment in the palace.*—ROSABELLA *sits in an armchair, plays the guitar or mandolin as the curtain rises. She then kisses the instrument, and says:*

Rosabella. Happy little friend, in my endless misery! How often you gladden the dreary heart, ever faithful companion of mine! [*Rises slowly.*] Oh, the nameless wretchedness of a blind creature! No ray of sunny lightness ever penetrates my heart; I wander in perpetual darkness. All the beauty that a loving Father has bestowed on earth and its children is unknown to me—night is day, and day is night, ever since I first breathed God's air in this valley of woe. Gladly would I exchange the princely splendor, that is said to surround me, for the humblest hovel of a peasant in the rugged mountains, could I receive sight. What enjoyment can this be for the blind Princess of Valencia? And what makes me more despondent, is the fact that I have saddened my parents' life. They were ashamed of me; my mother hides me away where no one ever dreams of my existence, except, perhaps, in a sympathetic allusion to the blind senorita. I have disgraced the proud line of the house of Valencia, though by no fault of mine. Since my father's death I am known, at least in law, as the heiress of these vast domains; but what use is all this to me? Oh, good God! is there no remedy for me? [*Sits down and weeps.*]

Enter LAURINDA.

Laurinda. Senorita in tears again! Why this sorrow, and why the tears?.

Rosabella. Nothing unusual, dear Laurinda; my old misery is crushing me again.

Laurinda. Shake off this despondency, Senorita; the Princess of Valencia need not weep.

Rosabella. If she is blind, others might weep for her.

Laurinda. Senorita speaks wisely; my heart is deeply moved at your wretchedness. Every hour of my life I compassionate the Princess.

Rosabella. I am aware of that, dear Laurinda, and your sympathy soothes and relieves; but she who most should love me, loves me the least—by her I am treated as an outcast in my own. Since my father's death, harshness increases, and I fear it will kill —

Laurinda. There is an All-avenging God, my Senorita. Providence may have happier days in store for you; your mother's heart may change—but change, it scarcely will!

Rosabella. Unless our common God will touch these closing lids, and bid me bathe my eyes in Shiloh's waters, that I may see—perhaps then—

Laurinda. Her own might open to see her malice; she is a wicked woman.

Rosabella. Laurinda, do not speak in such terms of the Princess, for she is my mother.

Laurinda. Yes, true, but has the Senorita heard her parent's last edict?

Rosabella. Speak, speak, Laurinda! What does it mean?

Laurinda. For Senorita to be transported to the royal asylum for the blind, and Lucilla to be sent to Madrid to attend school.

Rosabella. Why these sudden changes?

Laurinda. That Senora, the Princess of Valencia, may enjoy her life without the burden of a blind and feeblé maiden.

Rosabella. That is folly! Have I ever hindered any one's enjoyment? How could a poor blind girl do so?

Laurinda. By no fault of hers, to be sure.

Enters MINA.

Mina. Princess Rosabella, our august Senora commands that Lucilla be brought here; her ladyship desires to be present at an entertainment to be given in honor of the Duke of Cadiz, this evening.

Rosabella. If Senora, my mother commands, I joyfully obey. I shall be delighted to have my sister with me.

Mina. Very well, Senorita. [*Departs.*]

Rosabella. I am happy that Lucilla is permitted to come to me; we shall have a pleasant evening. But there is some one else whose company I would enjoy. [*Rings bell.*]

Enter ANTONIA.

Antonia. Senorita has called me?

Rosabella. Antonia, you will convey to my nurse, Gertrude, my highest esteem, and bid her visit me this evening.

Antonia. Pardon, Senorita, her ladyship has given contrary orders to me.

Rosabella. But not to Gertrude, so let a messenger run the errand as soon as her ladyship has departed.

Antonia. Very well.   [*Exit.*

Laurinda. How happy good Gertrude will be. But here comes Princess Lucilla.

Enter LUCILLA.

Lucilla. Good-evening, darling sister. [*Kisses her.*] I am very, very glad to be permitted to come to you this evening; I have a great piece of news to bring you.

Rosabella. I have heard it; Laurinda told me all.

Lucilla. Surely she has not heard what I have heard —something wonderful and great.

Rosabella. You are always living in fairy-lands, and bring me fairy-tales—to cheer me, no doubt.

Lucilla. But not this evening, sister; no fairy-tales these.

Rosabella. Then come and tell me.

[LUCILLA *leads* ROSABELLA *to a sofa.*]

Lucilla. The whole city is in excitement, sister, over an apparition of our Blessed Mother.

Rosabella [*makes the sign of the cross*]. Apparition of our Blessed Mother! Speak, child, speak!

Lucilla. Beyond the Pyrenees, sister, there is a small town near the borders of France and Spain—I relate it as correctly as I know and understand it—from here, perhaps, a hundred miles distant, they say. The place is called Lourdes. There, on the eleventh of February, just two weeks ago, our Blessed Mother appeared to a shepherd-girl, in the rocks of a cave. She is so beautiful and so grand, and speaks so lovingly — the Madonna. She has appeared nearly ten times to the same girl.

Rosabella. Where have you heard this news?

Lucilla. From Gertrude and her children—they were down in the city today—besides, the daily papers have it all.

Enter PRINCESS ELENORA, *unperceived.*

Laurinda. This will account for a passage in the letter I received today from my uncle, the Bishop of Tarbes, to which diocese Lourdes belongs.

[*She opens letter and reads.*]

"Great things are transpiring at Lourdes in these days, my Laurinda, if all is true—as I do not doubt. Heaven is smiling upon us and France."

Princess Elenora [*suddenly all are frightened*]. Great things, indeed, are transpiring here this evening; and I am fortunate in discovering the culprits. I wondered from whom my daughters receive their fair training in all the religious superstitions of the day; and now I have the source. I shall take heed that such communications are prevented in future. Laurinda Fountaine, your future service is no longer wanted in the castle. I give you one day to pack your fineries and laces, and to depart from here. And pack them well, for remember, the Princess of Valencia shall make your true character known in all Spain.

Laurinda. Your ladyship will pardon my interruption. Yes, I will go, and leave, at your command, your poor, neglected, blind daughter; but fear not that Laurinda Fountaine shall suffer want. The princely houses of Spain, save that of Valencia, are too Catholic to listen to such abuse as your ladyship will deign to heap upon me.

Elenora. Silencio! I am mistress here.

Laurinda. And I am no slave.

Elenora. Silencio, or else you leave this house to-night.

Laurinda. To find a brighter and happier home.

Elenora. Silencio! I command again; and you daughters, shall find other places, where the least spark of these superstitions will be wiped from your minds. For the night I leave you. Laurinda Fountaine, you go!

Laurinda. Adios, Senorita Rosabella, adios.

[*Bows and leaves.*

ELENORA *rings the bell violently.* ANTONIA *and* MINA *appear.*

Elenora. You are ordered to keep strict watch over these girls tonight. I may not return till after midnight.

Mina and Antonia. Very well, your ladyship.

[*Departs.*

Rosabella and Lucilla [*were crying during the violent burst of* ELENORA, *and sat closely together; now they arise and say sweetly and quietly:*] Good night, mamma, good night. [*She does not answer.*]

Rosabella. Poor, poor Laurinda.

Lucilla [*turning to the maids*]. We desire to be alone.

Rosabella. Antonia! You here?

Antonia. Yes, Senorita.

Rosabella. Do not forget my request — please.

Antonia. The messenger is dispatched.

Rosabella. Bring Gertrude at once to me, when she arrives.

Lucilla. Is Gertrude coming? Oh, she can tell all about the apparition! That's grand!

Rosabella. Go to your rooms, ladies, and when called come in haste.

Mina and Antonia. Yes, Senorita. [*Bow and depart.*

Lucilla. Now we are alone. I hear our mother's carriage passing [*looks*] through the court-yard; she is gone. Now listen, sister. It seems to be true that our Heavenly Mother is appearing in France. So many people are going there, even from Spain; and many miracles are wrought.

Rosabella. Oh! could that be so?

Lucilla. Yes, a fountain has appeared at the foot of the grotto; and the sick are healed — the lame walk, the blind see, the deaf hear.

Rosabella. Oh, darling sister! [*draws her closely to herself*]. Oh! could I go there, I know, I know that I would be healed!

Lucilla. Oh, that can easily be. Would you trust your little sister? [*Most affectionately.*] Rosabella, would you trust your little sister?

Rosabella. Willingly, joyfully!

Lucilla. If that is so, listen; let us leave the castle tonight—we can safely reach Gertrude's house without being seen—and tomorrow, early, before sunrise, the two little pilgrims will be on the way to Lourdes. You take your guitar, and both our heavy black cloaks. I know no one would recognize us, and no one harm us in Catholic Spain. Besides, we can reach Lourdes in five days.

Rosabella. But what would mother say?

Lucilla. She would be angry, of course; but it would not be the first time, and it soon will wear off. Besides, we return again; and if you come cured, she will be happy.

Rosabella. And we could pray to make her a good, pious woman, could we not? We could pray for her conversion; we could pray that she may love God again.

Lucilla. That we can. God's ways are wonderful; all might be accomplished.

Rosabella. But we cannot leave without money. See, Lucilla, how much is in my bank; here is the key.

Lucilla [*takes key, returns with bank and opens it*]. Oh, you are rich! Why, lots of gold in here—let me see [*counts money*]. This makes five hundred francs —plenty, plenty! [*Puts money in a pocket-book*].

Rosabella. So we need not suffer want; in ten days we ought to be home again. We must have conveyances, of course.

Lucilla. Leave all that to your little sister. You are blind, and I will be guide in this pilgrimage.

Rosabella. Oh, sweet little darling! our guardian angels will be with us [*tears roll down her cheeks*].

Enter GERTRUDE *with* AGNES.

Gertrude. Good evening, Senorita. Good evening, Rosabella. Oh, mi ninita, mi ninita! why dost thou cry?

Rosabella. Come, good Gertrude, take my hand [*takes and kisses it*]. Let me feel that you are here [*feels her face*]. Oh, you are so good! I am so glad you came—rest yourself.

[GERTRUDE *takes a chair close,* ROSABELLA *and* AGNES *standing.*]

Gertrude. I have always been a mother to thee; and watched thee like my own little Agnes, whom I nursed with thee in her babyhood.

Rosabella. Is Agnes here?

Gertrude. Yes, darling ninita, here is thy sister. Come, be not afraid.

[AGNES *takes* ROSABELLA'S *hand and kisses it.*]

Agnes. I pray that our good Princess is well.

Rosabella. Yes, Agnes, I am well — very well.

Gertrude. Thou hast always been well, ninita.

Rosabella. Yes, yes, but as "blind as a bat," they say.

Gertrude. I dreamt, last night, that I saw thee open thine eyes. I saw thee have beautiful eyes, Rosabella; and I saw thee look so happy and smile so sweetly.

Lucilla. Perhaps, Aunt Gertrude, all will yet come true.

Gertrude. God bless thy little heart, if it should happen.

Lucilla. Gertrude, tell my sister of the apparition of the Madonna at Lourdes.

Gertrude [*blesses herself*]. Yes, yes, I must tell thee that our dear Mother appeared at Lourdes; she comes nearly every day and speaks to a poor shepherd-girl. She has shown her a spring in a cave; and people wash their sick hands, or feet, or eyes in it, and they get well. Oh, if I had thee there, Rosabella, I believe my dream of thee would come true.

Lucilla. Suppose you let us go there, or help us get there.

Gertrude. How could I do that?

Lucilla. By helping us to leave the castle.

Gertrude. And what would her Highness, the Princess, say?

Lucilla. Miss us, of course; certainly not pray for us. But she is not home tonight, and we could easily escape.

· *Gertrude.* Tonight! Tonight!

Rosabella. Yes, tonight, dear Gertrude.

Gertrude. And who has given thee such an idea?

Rosabella [*arises*]. God, dear Gertrude, God; for I am convinced that He will cure me if I go to Lourdes.

Gertrude. But thou wouldst disobey thy mother, ninita.

Rosabella. If I follow God's voice, I disobey *no one;* and if I have your blessing and consent, Gertrude, I shall fear nothing. You have been to me a real mother. In my infant heart you implanted piety and love of God — from you I have all I so deeply cherish in my religion [*sits down again*].

Gertrude. Be quiet, ninita, be quiet! Hold thine little tongue! When thou wert only six months old, I carried thee with my Agnes, who is three days older than thou, to the castle chapel, and there I consecrated you both to our dear Lady; so thou art Mary's child indeed. Then thou art my ninita—then thou belongest to the Princess. But will thy little feet take thee to Lourdes?

Rosabella. We need not walk great distances; for I have money sufficient.

Agnes. Please, Senorita, take me along as a maid.

Lucilla. That's well, Agnes, you come with us—you can do many little things for us.

Gertrude. And when wilt thou start?

Rosabella. At once, Gertrude, at once. The Princess, my mother, will not reach the palace before one in the morning; she is with her ladies at the State reception of the Duke of Cadiz. Tomorrow, she and they will sleep till twelve at noon; so, possibly, she may ask for us by three in the afternoon—by that time, I hope we will have reached France.

Gertrude. Surely thou canst take the mail-coach at three, tomorrow morning — it is a warm, moonlight night — by ten thou art in France. In four days thou oughtest reach Lourdes. But thou must disguise thyself.

Lucilla. We all will [*rings the bell*].

Enter MINA.

Mina, please have our long, black cloaks and big hats sent to Gertrude's house at once — and this guitar. Having given that order, please return.

Mina. Very well, Senorita.

Rosabella. Mina, has Laurinda retired?

Mina. Yes, she feels ill, and was weeping.

Rosabella. Do not disturb her. [*Exit* MINA.] Poor Laurinda was discharged today, Gertrude; please keep her till we return from Lourdes. Then tell no one a word whither we are going; no one is to know where we are [*they rise*].

Gertrude. Indeed, thou mayest trust me, ninita. But if thou returnest without being cured?

Rosabella. My confidence is unshaken, Gertrude. There is no possibility of such an alternative.

Gertrude. Thou dost have faith, daughter, strong enough to move a mountain.

Lucilla. Let us go, in the name of God. We will stay with you, Aunt Gertrude, till tomorrow, then Agnes will depart with us.

ROSABELLA *rings the bell twice.* MINA *and* ANTONIA *enter.*

Rosabella. Mina and Antonia, are you here?

Both. Yes, Senorita.

Rosabella. One request your poor, unfortunate, blind mistress makes today. My sister and I are going on a mission — strange, indeed, but holy; mysterious, yet certain. I beg you, console our mother if she should grow sad for having lost her daughters; they shall surely return.

Both. Can it be possible! Can it be possible!

Rosabella. I shall reward both of you on my return; and I assure you, our castle will then be a happy home.

Both. May God be blessed! But you should not go.

Rosabella. I must; so adios, dear girls, adios.

Both. ·May God protect you, then, Senorita. [*Depart.*

Gertrude. And may thy holy Guardian Angel be thy guide on the way. Let me bless you, child, instead of your mother [*makes the sign of the cross on her forehead*], for I have been thy mother. Fear nothing. On the way to Lourdes, speak to *no* one — tell no one thy story. Kiss the picture of thy mother [*kisses the pic-*

ture], and take this medal, that nothing may harm thee. When thou comest to Lourdes, pray much and do not despair — God will help thee!

Rosabella. Come then, my sisters [*takes* AGNES *and* LUCILLA *by the hand*], and let us consecrate our Pilgrimage. [*All three kneel down. No light.*]

GUARDIAN ANGEL *appears, touches them on the shoulder and leads them away.*

CURTAIN.

ACT III

SCENE.—*Grotto of Lourdes as in the First Act.—Rustic benches in front.—The cave closed off by a rope stretched across the stage and marked with a prohibition.—Fountain, or moss-covered basin holding water, in the cave.—*LUCILLA, AGNES *and* ROSABELLA *enter as the curtain rises, walking slowly; the former leads* ROSABELLA.—*The three children wear pilgrim cloaks and large, black felt hats.*

Lucilla. This must be the place, Agnes.

Agnes. I hardly think we mistook the path shown us by the kind ladies, Senorita; this is to the right of the river, and here is the rocky cave.

Lucilla. Of course we are right. Come, Rosabella, here is a bench; rest yourself.

Rosabella. Are we in the sacred grotto? Tell me, Lucilla, does it represent the picture in my dream?

Lucilla. Surely, sister. But your dream was so indistinct, your cave was gloomy; but here is life and sunshine.

Rosabella. Believe me, Lucilla, my little body feels that I am in a sacred spot. Oh, let me kiss the ground! [*bends down.*]

Lucilla. No, no; we might be mistaken.

Rosabella. No, we are *not;* I assure you we are not! Where is my rosary?

Agnes. On your left arm, Senorita.

Rosabella. Thanks, thanks. Are we alone?

Lucilla [*looks*]. There is no one here but you, Agnes and I; yet I thought I heard voices — yes, there are ladies ascending the path towards the cave. They appear to be women of prominence.

Rosabella. And where shall we find Bernadette?

Lucilla. That I cannot say; but if you are content to remain here by yourself, we will go and find Bernadette. Do you fear to remain alone?

Rosabella. Fear? Fear what, Lucilla? How could fear enter my mind in this place; and then my Guardian Angel will protect me and stand at my side. I fear not even darkness, for I exist in darkness, Lucilla; and my rosary shall entertain me while you are gone. So make haste and bring Bernadette to me. Tell her a poor, blind girl asks her prayers and her assistance. Make haste! Seek the child of Mary, and bring Heaven's favored one to me.

Lucilla. We will go. Recite your rosary; and if these ladies should come here, speak not a word to them, for I notice a prohibition on the railing — they might be ill disposed, and hurt our cause.

Rosabella. You are a sweet little woman. I will do as you say; but make haste.

Lucilla. Adios, sister [*kisses her*].

Agnes. Adios, Senorita [*kisses her hand*].

[*Exeunt.*

Rosabella [*alone*]. Alone again—alone with myself and God's holy angel. How faithful that dear Guardian Angel has been to us! He has brought us hither through a thousand dangers.

[GUARDIAN ANGEL *appears in the background.*]

Like Tobias, he has safely conducted me into a foreign land; he has brought me to Mary's sacred abode. [*Rises and kneels, facing the grotto.*] Mother of Mercy, help thy poor child who, pleading, kneels at thy shrine; open my dead, sightless orbs, let me see God's beauty in fair nature! Dispel this darkness—dismal, dreary, frightful.

[GUARDIAN ANGEL, *points towards the fountain.*]

Thou hast given earthly life to Him through whom light came into this world. Mother, I speak as a child, hear my prayer. To thee I cry from this valley of tears. Truly, I might be more miserable than I am. Born a grandee of Spain, I have been reared in affluence. Gladly will I share of my abundance with God's poor; and to thee, Mary, I promise, if my mortal eyes be opened and if thy Son's grace touch the spiritual eyes of my unfortunate mother, to aid in the erection of the magnificent temple which shall crown this hill and forever consecrate these rocks. This, dear Mother Immaculate, is thy poor child's vow; receive it, but let me see — let me see!

[*Weeps, while little angels surround her, who quickly withdraw to the cave as she rises, and facing the grotto, sings:*

> Ave Sanctissima,
>   In pity lend thine ear,
> Ora pro me,
>   My hymn of pleading hear.
> From heaven, eternal bend;
>   Mother, give thy blind child sight,
> Dispel this cloud, this darkness rend,
>   O, give me light!
> Star of earth's pilgrim weak,
>   In thy tender mercy guide;
> Grant the boon I seek!

[*Refrain by the angels.*]

> Sweet Mother, sweet Mother, hear,
> Ora pro ea,
> Thou star of radiance great,
> Ora Mater, Ora, Queen Immaculate.

[*Voices are heard. The angels disappear, singing as they depart.*]

Enter MADAME MASSAY, *wife of the Governor of Hautes-Pyrenees,* MADAME DR. DOZONS *and* MADEMOISELLE VERGEZ, *talking.*

Mme. Massay. In accordance with an imperial decree, Baron Massay has strictly prohibited any approach to the cave. It seems that these poor, ignorant

villagers are shamefully deceived by this young mischief of a girl. One can scarcely believe that so much
deceit, such cunning and such plausible stories could .
be invented by a girl who hardly knows how to read
and write, and has spent most of her days on the mountains with the cows and sheep. Believe me, Madame
Dozons, there is some deep and wicked plot in all this.
I have promised the Governor that, on my visit to
Lourdes, I would inspect the place myself, and give a
faithful account of what I see here.

Mme. Dozons. I must ask leave to disagree with
your Ladyship. I see no reason why all that has happened here should be deceit.   .

Mme. Massay. Poor, deluded creature, I see your
convent education always gets the upper hand. You
ought to have Sisters Genevieve and Madelaine here
with you; and I would not be surprised if each of you
would see a lady—one white, the other black, I suppose.

Mlle. Verges. Please, aunt, do not mock holy things
in such a way. God will punish you.

Mme. Massay. No, no, dear Julia, no danger. I
have a great big faith in my heart, but I do hate
deceit. Now listen; did you ever have a dream?

Mlle. Verges. Why, certainly!

Mme. Massay. And you believed everything you
dreamt?

Mlle. Verges. Why, no!

Mme. Massay. Well, this mischief, Bernadette, is a
dreamer, with the difference that she dreams with eyes
wide open and you with eyes closed.

Mme. Dozons. Happy dreams she dreams only; some people whose eyes were closed have opened through her dreams.

[ROSABELLA *coughs.*]

Mme. Massay. Why, some one must be here. [*Looks about and sees* ROSABELLA.] Well, well, a little bundle of clothes wrapt around a poor blind girl. What do you want here? Where do you come from?

[ROSABELLA *apparently weeps. No answer.*]

Mme. Dozons and Mlle. Vergez. Perhaps the poor creature is deaf.

Mme. Massay. Is she from Lourdes?

Mme. Dozons. I have never seen her in our town.

Mme. Massay. A stranger then. I wonder whether she read the prohibition?

Mme. Dozons. Why, certainly; if she is as blind as a bat.

Mlle. Vergez. You ask so many foolish questions,

Mme. Massay. She will be arrested. I think she is letting on. Wait! I know how to try these poor, blind, deaf creatures.

[*Takes out a coin and puts it in* ROSABELLA'S *hand. She throws it over her head into the cave.*]

Ha! Ha! There is something mysterious in this being; she must belong to the vision. Perhaps we will soon hear a new description of the so-called "White Lady."

Mlle. Vergez. She is teaching you a lesson, aunt, by throwing the coin towards the cave; she means that all that is given here should be given to Mary.

Mme. Massay. Well! Well! A wonderfully logical head you have! I shall beg my husband, the Governor, to nominate Mademoiselle Vergez alms collector for the would-be shrine at Lourdes.

Mlle. Vergez. And let me assure you, my Lady, that it will not be many, many months when her Ladyship, the Governoress of Hautes-Pyrenees, will send to this shrine a substantial contribution.

Mme. Massay. Great is Israel in her prophets! surely I have given my share; for a franc-piece is lying yonder. But I must say, this girl is really blind.

Mlle. Vergez. But not deaf, for I see a significant smile upon those childish lips. Let me ask. Are you blind, Mademoiselle?

Rosabella. Yes, Senorita [*smiles sweetly*].

Mme. Massay. Ha! she is Spanish. How does she know that you are a young Senorita, if she is blind?

Mlle. Vergez. Without doubt by my words, dear aunt. Sister Antonia used to tell us children that all women are foolish when they marry, so perhaps this Spanish lass can wisely distinguish between the married Senora and the unmarried Senorita.

Mme. Massay. Thank you, Senorita Julia; you are well brought up.

Mlle. Vergez. And equal to any task.

Mme. Massay. Enough of this now. I pity this poor blind child and wonder how she came here, and what she wants here anyway.

Mme. Dozons. Nothing less than her eyesight, I presume.

Mme. Massay. Then she should consult your husband, the doctor.

Mme. Dozous. He might tell her to do what she herself intends to do.

Mme. Massay. What is that?

Mme. Dozous. Bathe her eyes in yonder water.

Mme. Massay. You mean to say that so intelligent and cultured a gentleman as your husband believes in these proceedings here?

Mme. Dozous. Exactly. He is convinced. This morning the poor blind quarryman, who lost his eyesight some ten years ago, came to him perfectly cured; and all by this water, which his young daughter brought him.

Mme. Massay. Well, well! That is strange.

Mlle. Verges. Yes; our Lord Bishop has now the case, and many similar ones, in hand; if decides in favor of the apparition, no civil power can hinder the people from coming here.

Mme. Massay. That he won't, that he won't; he is too shrewd a man. Not even the Curé of Lourdes has been here.

Mme. Dozous. But he has sent messages to the "White Lady," and she in turn to him.

Mme. Massay. It is easy to convey messages when you have no assurance of their delivery. Bernadette plays her part well.

Mme. Dozous. Bernadette, Madame, is the Lily of the Pyrenees; though of humble parentage she possesses qualities that would adorn a Queen. She is an angel among the children of her age. Since her return from the mountains, I have watched her carefully; her piety is admired and her simplicity charms. I can assure you, Madame, that Bernadette is no fraud; she is incapable of deceit.

Mme. Massay. A noble champion of the shepherdess! Surely the Governor will be delighted to learn of this turn of events.

Mme. Dozons. Still greater ones will happen, Madame, ere the sun has set thirty times from today.

Mme. Massay. Yes, the whole village will be in a state of excitement; frenzy will reign supreme, and superstition hold its sway. A bright future for the peaceful valley of the Pyreness. But why lose patience? I have seen enough and heard enough to convince me that radical measures must be taken to protect the people in our province. Let us go. [*Approaches* ROSA-BELLA *and shakes her by the shoulder.*] Child, you are forbidden to stay here; the decree is issued and must be obeyed!

Rosabella. Yes, Senora.

Mlle. Vergez. Don't trouble the poor child. Let the Lord Governor come and arrest the poor, blind creature if he dare.

Mme. Dozons. Some one will surely come for her. Madame, let us remain in the vicinity and watch the outcome.

Mme. Massay. It strikes me that I passed a band of gypsies, on the highway from the city to Lourdes, today. Do you think she is one?

Mme. Dozons. She has not the appearance; but gypsy or no gypsy, let us leave her. I hope she will not attempt to walk by herself, for she might fall into the river.

Mme. Massay. And drown; then we would have a tragedy added to the comedy. [*Exeunt to the side.*

Enter AGNES *and* LUCILLA *with* BERNADETTE. *They have watched the ladies depart.*

Lucilla [*behind the stage*]. They are gone. Oh, dear sister, we are here at last! We were gone a long, long time, and you must have been nearly frightened to death.

> [BERNADETTE *stands at a distance unmindful of all, and with folded hands gazes pensively at the cave.*]

Rosabella. Some women were here, and one was very cross. She said she did not believe in the apparition. They made me feel very sad; she called Bernadette a fraud. [*slowly*]. Did you bring her?

Lucilla. Surely, sister; she is here.

Rosabella [*animated*]. Oh! where is she? [*Stretches out her hands.*] Oh! where is she??

Lucilla [*walks to* BERNADETTE *and brings her to* ROSABELLA]. My blind sister, Bernadette.

Bernadette. God bless you, kind friend [*gives her her hand*].

Rosabella [*kisses the hand devoutly*]. Oh, happy moment of my life to be with you! Blessed the hour!

Bernadette. Do not speak so; I am only a poor mountain lass.

Rosabella [*tries to find the other hand and puts both to her cheeks, so as to touch the eyes*]. Oh, blessed, blessed, thrice blessed Bernadette! You are heaven's favored child; you have seen our heavenly Mother! Oh, pray [*beseechingly*] to our good Lady that I may see, that poor Rosabella may see!

Bernadette. God's Mother can help you, for she has helped many.

Rosabella. And I am sure she will help me.

Bernadette. Have you prayed to her?

Rosabella. Every day, sweet Bernadette; and on my way hither we prayed nearly all the time. See my rosary, it feels as though it was badly worn.

Bernadette. And how far did you come?

Rosabella. From Spain, Bernadette.

Bernadette. From Spain? That must be very far.

Lucilla. From San Sebastiano, in Spain—about one hundred miles from here.

Bernadette. Who spoke to you of Lourdes?

Agnes. My parents have heard the wonderful stories.

Rosabella. Yes, Gertrude has told us all.

Bernadette. She told you of Lourdes?

Rosabella. Yes, and of Bernadette.

Bernadette. And then you left home and came here?

Rosabella. Yes.

Bernadette. With your parents' permission?

Rosabella. My father is dead and my mother knows nothing of our whereabouts.

Bernadette. So you came without her consent? Oh, I fear you have done wrong! I fear all our prayers will be of no avail. Our Blessed Mother will not listen to us.

Rosabella. She will not? [*Sadly.*] Bernadette, she will not? Oh! what will become of me? [*weeps*]

> [AGNES *and* LUCILLA *turn away, looking very sad.*]

What shall I do? Tell me, Bernadette.

Bernadette. Return home and ask your mother's blessing.   ·   .

Rosabella. Oh, Bernadette, I cannot, I cannot! She hates me, she despises me; her blessing she would and could not give, for there is little faith in her heart. Bernadette [*kneels before her*], gladly—oh! believe me —would I remain blind all the days of my life if my darling mother's spiritual eyes were opened, if the stony heart would soften through the influence of love and religion. Let us pray, dear Bernadette; let us pray at least for my mother.

> [BERNADETTE *helps her to arise.*]

Bernadette. Do not kneel before me; this place is consecrated to God's Mother. Rosabella, beautiful rose —for this seems to be your name—do you love your mother?

Rosabella. With my whole heart. She is my mother, and that tells all.

Bernadette. Are these your sisters?

Rosabella. One is, Lucilla; the other—yes, she, too is my sister, for from her mother I received both spiritual and earthly food; yes, she is my sister. Her mother's blessings and prayers are with us, and every moment, no doubt, she thinks of us. She, in the simplicity of her heart, has entrusted us to the care of our holy Guardian Angel. He has stood by our side, and he will lead us safely back to our home and to our own.

Bernadette. You speak nobly, girl, and I see your heart is filled with faith. I will pray to our good Mother for you. Go, then, to the fountain, while I kneel in prayer [*points to the fountain, but sees the obstruction .* But, ah! they have closed the fountain! When will the good people believe me? Mary has given a heavenly sign, and they are again deceiving themselves.

Rosabella. Do not leave me, Bernadette. Will any one harm you or us?

Bernadette. I fear nothing, Rosabella, only sin. But they may harm you.

Rosabella. They cannot harm us, dear Bernadette. Has the Virgin Mother ever spoken to you?

Bernadette [*animated*]. Yes, she spoke words of heavenly sweetness, and in a tone so sad, so sad. France, beautiful France, must do penance, else God's hand will rest heavily upon her. She demands that a chapel be built in this place.

Rosabella. A chapel! A chapel! No, a church shall be built here, and I will help; I have vowed it to our Blessed Mother.

Bernadette. Oh! you poor, blind child, Rosabella.

Rosabella. I am blind, Bernadette, hence poor; but my life is a mystery to you. Take me to the fountain; after I see I will tell you all.

[LUCILLA *and* AGNES, *with* BERNADETTE, *tear down the prohibition and railing.*]

Bernadette. Do not fear, Rosabella, Mary will hear

your prayers. Oh! how sweetly she smiled when I asked her to cause the rose bush to bloom in the cave, as I was commanded to do by our dear Pastor, the Curé. She smiled and she pointed to that spot, then dry and rocky. With my hands I scratched away the surface soil, and behold! a fountain of crystal water bubbled up; and believe me, sister, hundreds have been cured by the use of the miraculous water.

> [*Points to the water and begs* AGNES *and* LUCILLA *to go there with* ROSABELLA. *She herself feels the happy moment of a new apparition approach, and becomes radiant with joy.*]

The dewy shades of evening are fast falling, the sun is sinking into the arms of the invisible.

> [*All look at her with astonishment.*]

Heaven smiles again upon me. Rosabella—go—to—the—fountain—bathe—your—eyes—now—blind—call upon—our—loving—Mother—in—Heaven—pray—to—her—and—you—shall—see.

[*Angelus bell rings; she falls on her knees. Children go to the fountain and kneel. Soft music. Apparition appears.* BERNADETTE *in ecstasy. They bathe* ROSABELLA'S *eyes, slowly, carefully and with devotion, then take a silk handkerchief and hold it over the eyes of the blind girl while praying silently. Red light burns.* ROSABELLA *gradually takes away the bandage, wipes her face and eyes, looks about for a moment, as if dazed, and runs to the front of the stage, seemingly unmindful of the others. For stage effect,* ROSABELLA *may open her black cloak, while kneeling at the grotto, so that her princely garments may be seen, thereby improving her appearance in the outburst of joy. Her hat falls back on her shoulders. She says:*]

Rosabella. Joy! Joy! I see! I see! The night is over, the day is come! Can this be Heaven? Surely so fair a realm must be tenanted by angels; or am I just outside the golden gates? Yes, yes, 'tis true! See yonder, where the earth meets sky, a wondrous, dazzling glory surrounds a fiery disc; a golden light bathes this mysterious land, long rays of light sweep over the grass and trees. Ah! now I recall: 'tis the sun bidding farewell to the earth. Oh! the ecstasy which thrills my heart! I gaze upon this scene as one might gaze having never known its like before. I scarce dare move or speak; but drink its sweetness down into my soul. No sound breaks the silence, and thus I stand, in rapture, beholding the vision of a God-created world. How merciful thou art, O Mary, thy blind child knows! Thou hast stooped from Heaven to touch these sightless orbs, which have never looked upon the world before, and given them the precious boon of sight. Every blade of grass sings to me; the flowers, swaying in the breeze, wave a "Te Deum." Ah! who is this sweet, young being? Surely—yes, it must be my own dear, little sister, small no longer — larger than I imagined—but yet as fair as the blossoms; and this saintly looking creature, who seems not of the earth!

[*While* ROSABELLA *speaks,* LUCILLA *and* AGNES *stand in attitudes of amazement.* BERNADETTE *continues in prayer during* ROSABELLA'S *outburst of joy. Finally,* LUCILLA *calls her sister.*]

Lucilla. Sister, sister, is it true or a dream?

Rosabella. Oh, my darling sister! no dream; reality, reality. I see, I see!

> [*Embraces* LUCILLA, *and turning to* AGNES, *pats her on the cheek, saying:*]

Good, kind Agnes, oh, how happy this moment! the sweetest of my life; for life, for me, is but just beginning. And now where is our dear Bernadette?

Lucilla. Still in ecstasy and prayer.

> [BERNADETTE *waking as though from a dream.* ROSABELLA *rushes to her in joy.*]

Rosabella. Oh, Bernadette! Bernadette! I see. Tell me, tell me, have I opened my eyes in Heaven?

Bernadette. No, 'tis the earth, and although you hear no angels' songs, *you* must glorify and thank her who appeared to me and gave you sight. A sign, testifying that the apparition is supernatural, has again been given us; and you must be ever grateful to the Mistress of Heaven for the great blessing she has bestowed upon you. Return to your home; your sight has been received, there remains but the spiritual blindness of your mother.

Rosabella. I go; but not many weeks shall pass ere you see me again. Then shall be revealed to you my name and position in life. One favor more I beg of you, O Bernadette, powerful advocate with Mary— pray to her for my poor, perverted mother.

MME. MASSAY, MME. DOZONS *and* MLLE. VERGEZ
rush from their hiding places, saying:

And pray for us, Bernadette; pray for us.

Mme. Massay. Great is the mystery transacted before our eyes this hour! Great is "Our Lady of Lourdes."

[ROSABELLA *embraces* BERNADETTE.]

CURTAIN.

ACT IV

SCENE.—*Apartment in the castle.*—GERTRUDE, *sitting in a comfortable chair, working on some embroidery;* STELLA *and* TERESA *at her feet, the latter with a book of fairy tales.*—*Table and other furniture to either side of the stage.*

Teresa [*breaking off reading*]. Mamma, after school today, I did what you told me this morning.

Gertrude. That's an obedient girl. Good children always do as they are told.

Stella. Suppose they would not?

Gertrude. Then they deserve to be punished—one —two—three—and if you disobey—four—five—six— you certainly shall be—seven—eight.

Teresa. What are you counting, mamma?

Gertrude. Stitches on my work—nine—ten—eleven.

Teresa [*on her fingers*]. You missed ten, mamma.

Gertrude. Be quiet, or else I shall make a mistake.

Stella [*arises and watches her*]. How many stitches in a row, mamma?

Gertrude. Don't disturb me; go out on the veranda

and see whether any one is coming. .I am strangely uneasy this afternoon.

[STELLA *dances and exits.*

Teresa. Mamma, you did not mind what I said before [*stands up before her*].

Gertrude. And what is it darling? [*Puts her work aside*]. Tell mamma everything.

Teresa. See the lovely medal I received in school today, for being a good little girl; and then, when school was over, I went to the Church of San Sebastiano and prayed at the altar of our Senora for our dear blind Princess and Sister Agnes.

Gertrude [*brushing a tear from her eyes*]. A good, good child; and what does your little heart think of the Princess?

Teresa. That she will return. I dreamt, last night, that she would return and open her beautiful eyes. I saw her with a lovely angel near. She laid a white cloth over her blind eyes, and when it was removed she saw.

Gertrude. A delightful dream. Do you think it will come true?

Teresa. Yes, yes, mamma; look [*shows her book*]. I have just read the legend of St. Ottilia; she was a blind Princess of Lorraine, and became a Christian. A holy Bishop baptized her and prayed over her, and her eyes were opened, which made her mother very, very happy.

Gertrude. Well, well, darling, you are teaching your mamma [*takes her upon her lap*]. And what would you do if the Princess were to return cured of her blindness?

Teresa [*folding her little hands*]. I would thank God every hour of my life, and every day bring her the sweetest flowers I could find in the garden.

Gertrude. You did that when she was blind.

Teresa. Then [*reaches in her pocket*] I would say my rosary every day, to the saint who cured her.

Gertrude. Do saints cure?

Teresa. Yes, they can, through God who loves them dearly.

Gertrude. That's a good child [*kisses her*]. Now go and look for your sister.

[TERESA *jumps up and departs.*

Gertrude [*arises and looks after her*]. Happy children—my treasures, my joy. Little do they apprehend the trouble. Soon I shall have to leave this peaceful place, and where shall I find shelter for me and mine? The Princess is a raving maniac; since her children are gone she has lost all control of herself. I promised Rosabella to conceal her flight; but if they do not return today I shall go to the Princess, throw myself upon my knees and confess all. I will suffer—suffer as I deserve. Yet there is a loving Father watching over us; His will be done. He feeds the birds of the air, the beasts of the field; He will protect me and mine [*walks up and down, and looks through the window*]. I wonder what has come of Laurinda? She has persistently remained in the house so as not to come in contact with the Princess. If she learns that I have stored Laurinda away, there will be no hope for poor

Gertrude. My husband, Carlo, has been most faithful to the house of Valencia; but I fear we will have to look for other quarters — poor Carlo. Well, let me work. [*Takes up work*]. One, two, three, four—

Enter LAURINDA *and* ISABELLA.

Laurinda. Good evening, Gertrude. Ha! you certainly must have thought the bird had escaped—no, no, my wings are clipped, at least for the present, and I will have to be your boarder for another week. I had bad news, this afternoon, in a letter from my uncle— but, Gertrude, here is a lady with the best of news.

Isabella. Guess from whom.

Gertrude. From the Princess.

Isabella. Not from the one up there in the Alcazar, to be sure; but I do believe I have good news from the blind Princess.

Gertrude. From the blind Princess? [*smiles*].

Laurinda. Good little soul, I know you are happy; your thoughts are constantly "of thine little ninita."

Gertrude. Ninita; yes, mine ninita.

Enter STELLA *and* TERESA.

Teresa. See, mamma, what lovely roses Stella and I gathered in the Alameda. I shall keep them for the Princess Rosabella.

Gertrude. Are you so sure they will return soon?

[STELLA *puts flowers in the vase on the table.*]

Isabella. Perhaps this paper will give you information.

Gertrude. What paper?

Isabella. The "Voice of Truth"; here, read.

Gertrude. Wait, you know I cannot read without glasses [*looks for them*]. I wonder where they are.

Teresa. There, mamma, on your head.

Gertrude. Sure enough; you little mite, you see everything — yes, I am getting old and forgetful.

Stella. And gray—

Teresa. See, mamma, lots of gray hairs on your head [*looks for them*]. May I pull them out?

Stella [*strikes* TERESA's *little hand*]. Hush now, Teresa; let mamma read.

Gertrude [*takes paper, looks it over and returns it to* ISABELLA]. You better read; my eyes are weak, anyway.

Isabella. Listen: "Lourdes, France, March 4th, 1858. The supposed apparitions in the grotto continue —the excitement in the Provinces increases. Baroness Massay visited the spot, a few days ago, and reports to have witnessed a miracle. A blind girl, and supposed to have been a gypsy, received her eyesight upon the application of the water—"

Teresa and Stella]*clap their hands*]. That was the Princess!

Gertrude. But she is no gypsy .

Isabella. Silencio—"Were it not for the high position of Her Excellency, Madame Massay, the event could hardly be believed. The fact, however, is authenticated by a poor quarryman, known in this town as Louis Bouriette, who lost his eyes, twenty years ago, in a powder explosion, and now sees after applying the water. A paralyzed woman was carried to the grotto yesterday; today, is seen walking the streets. Wonder-

ful events are surely transpiring." Again: "Paris,
March 4th. His Imperial Majesty, Napoleon III, has
today dispatched a special commissioner to Lourdes to
investigate the apparitions and supposed miracles. His
Majesty awaits results with great uneasiness."

Gertrude. Well—well—what shall I say to all this?

Laurinda. Dates correspond with the time the Princess might have reached **Lourdes**.

Gertrude. But it says a poor gypsy girl. Rosabella
is no gypsy and is not poor.

Stella. ·Well, mamma, you know newspapers always
lie in something.

Isabella. The Princess may have traveled as a poor
girl. Gertrude, is there any news from the Alcazar?
Does her ladyship know where her children are?

Gertrude. Mina was here today. She described the
scenes in the castle—one storm after another; and all
the blame rests on me. Well, I have broad shoulders,
and by good Carlo consoles me by saying the storm
will pass. I only wish the Princess Rosabella would
return before we are driven away.

Isabella. Driven away!

Gertrude. I expect the sad news every moment. I
am praying for a home somewhere. We certainly have
always had luxurious apartments here—a happy home
—but worries will come, and must come, to the best
of us.

Laurinda. You are right, Gertrude; but when they
come they are hard to bear.

[*A tambourine heard.*]

Gertrude. Go, children, see what that means.

[*Exeunt* STELLA *and* TERESA.

Now, Laurinda, what is your cross?

Laurinda. My uncle writes that, at present, he knows of no vacancy in any noble family. But I cannot remain here; and if Rosabella does not return by tomorrow, I leave in the evening.

Isabella. Foolish girl, you can come to me if you are afraid to remain here.

Enter STELLA *and* TERESA.

Stella and Teresa. Oh! mamma—a little gypsy girl is outside on the Esplanade.

Teresa. She plays and dances lovely [*tries to imitate her*]. Let us call her in, mamma.

Gertrude. Certainly; we need a little amusement.

Stella [*calling outside.*] Come in, little gypsy maiden.

LYDIA *enters, playing and dancing a quickstep. Music. She bows gracefully when finished.*

Lydia. Senora and Senoritas, I am a poor gypsy girl, wandering about the world, homeless and friendless.

Gertrude. Where were you born?

Lydia. In fair Granada. I dwelt in the golden orange groves of the Alhambra, danced in the Alcazar of proud Sevilla, now to beg from door to door. I tell fortunes and sing lovely songs [*catches some one's hand*].

Laurinda. Where are your parents?

Lydia. My father, I know not; he is buried under

an olive tree at Cadiz. My mother I lost in the Sierra Nevada, so they say.

Isabella. Who say?

Lydia. The gypsies, of course, with whom I tramped through the world. They killed my·mother and stole me. They took me beyond the Pyrenees, where I escaped. They were wicked. Finally I came to Sebastiano.

Teresa [*walks up to* LYDIA *and looks at her with confidence*]. Little gypsy, you say you can tell fortunes. You know what we do not; tell us what has become of the blind Princess.

Lydia [*astonished, looks about*]. Blind Princess! blind Princess! [*takes a rose from the vase and holds it up after she has kissed it*].

> "Rosabella, beautiful rose,
> Lucilla, light ever as bright,
> Rosabella is now Lucilla
> She sees, she sees, dear Senorita,
> She bathed her eyes in the waters,
> In the waters of Massabielle,
> Oh happy, oh happy Rosabella."

[*Touches tambourine and dances.*]

All [*very astonished*]. How do you know that?
Lydia.

> The roses can speak, Senorita,
> They speak to me of Ninita.

[*Large bell rings.*]

Gertrude. Oh, nostra Senora! Oh, the Princess is coming from the castle. [*Bell rings.*] Go—go, children — ladies — go — here, gypsy [*gives her a coin*], hide yourself.

[*Bell rings again. They all leave. Someone takes*
Lydia, *who dances once or twice, laughing as
she departs.*]

Lydia.
> "La Princessa will love Rosabella,
> Rosabella will love la Princessa."
>
> [*Exeunt.*

Enter Princess of Valencia *with her ladies, who
stop at a distance.* Gertrude *meets her at the door,
bowing gracefully.*

Gertrude. Her ladyship is welcome to my apartments.

Princess [*sitting in a chair*]. Gertrude, I have come
on a matter of the greatest importance. You may sur-
mise what I am about to say, and you may have been
surprised that I have not come ere this. To be short, it
almost breaks my heart to learn that those who have
always shared my royal bounty should so far forget
themselves as to conspire in robbing me of my peace.

Gertrude. They deserve to be imprisoned.

Princess. You are pronouncing sentence upon yourself, woman. You have been the recipient of my favors,
you have surrounded yourself with all the comforts and
luxuries of life; and silently I bowed assent to all this.
You receive visits and make them in San Sebastiano.

Gertrude. Senora, you are misinformed. How could
I, a poor, clumsy, ignorant woman, play the lady in
aristocratic San Sebastiano? All know Gertrude.

Princess. You are speaking the truth. They know
you as a selfish, domineering, meddling woman. They
know you — and that means they do not respect you.

Gertrude. You speak wisely, noble Senora, but I fear your informers must have been mistaken.

Princess. Another piece of impertinence.

Gertrude. Surely you would not accuse me of all you said?

Princess. And more yet, woman, were I not to lower myself in noticing you at all.

Gertrude. True nobility, Senora, is found only in the heart; in this a princess and a beggar may be alike.

Princess. Do not speak thus in my presence.

Gertrude. My relation to your child, Senora, permits me to utter these sentiments—you accuse me falsely and I must defend myself. It may be well for you, even though you are the proud Princess of Valencia, to listen to a few words spoken truthfully and honestly, though spoken by your keeper's wife.

Princess [*arises*]. Be silent. I command. You have decoyed my children into your house and aided them in leaving their home; you are harboring one whom I have forbidden inside my doors, and in my madness I feel like piercing your infamous heart. Would that I were a man, you should even now be lying dead before me. [*In complete madness and hysterical.*] You are a shame to womankind, a disgrace to your sex, an outcast from society!

STELLA *and* TERESA *enter, crying.*

Mamma, come; do not stay here.

[PRINCESS *sees* STELLA *and takes her hysterically into her arms.*]

Princess. Come—come—you are partly my daughter.

[*Looks at her.*] Agnes, Agnes—no, you are not Agnes [*pushes her away*]. Go, go — all of you — leave my castle — leave my house —

Children [*fall on their knees*]. Do not be so cross, kind Princess; do not send us away.

Princess [*overcome, falls back into the chair and has a violent spell of weeping, and cries at times:*] Go — I say — go.

Gertrude [*who has retreated somewhat, now approaches calmly and motions to the children*]. Go, children, go. [*They depart. She kneels before the* PRINCESS, *smoothing her temples.*] I know you loved me once, noble Princess, and I shall not reprove you. I shall only speak as a mother speaks to a mother.

Princess. Speak, Gertrude, speak! Oh, my temples burst!

Gertrude. God has sent you this visitation because you have not loved your afflicted child. God has permitted this; something tells me so. You must be a good mother to your children, you must teach them to honor and love their religion. You belong to a proud Catholic race; your ancestors and your name are among the most revered grandees of the State. The noble blood of a Columbus flows in your veins—Catholic Columbus. Promise God, if your children return, you will be a good mother to them — promise now.

Princess. Gertrude [*hesitates, then amidst tears*], I promise faithfully and upon my honor.

Gertrude. Promise that you will love them. You have learned what it means to be without them. Promise upon your honor.

Princess [*slowly*]. Yes, I will love them.

Gertrude. Then, surely, God will lead them back to you. Return to your castle [*arises*], noble Princess, and believe me, your children are safe. Mina, Antonia [*approach*], the Princess is ill; lead her to the apartment on the left until she recovers.

Princess [*slowly rises with assistance*]. Gertrude, I will see you before I return to the castle. Adios.

[*Exeunt.*

Gertrude [*bows*]. Adios. What a miracle is wrought in that proud woman's heart! [*Kneels in the middle of the stage.*] Thanks, Heavenly Father, for this favor; now bid her children return.

CHILDREN *enter with* ISABELLA *and* LAURINDA.

Children. Is she gone? Oh, mother, must we leave?

Gertrude. Never, dear little mites; not until these massive walls fall.

Isabella. Is the storm over?

Gertrude. Calm is restored; the Princess is ill and has retired. But what is up again? [*Tambourine and guitar are heard.*] See who is out, Stella.

[STELLA *goes out.*

Surely the poor gypsy has not brought her whole tribe.

STELLA *returns with* LYDIA. LYDIA *bows.*

Lydia. May I ask the kind lady for a night's lodging for my companions and myself?

Gertrude. That's too much — too much. I gave you a franc, and here is another [*gives coin on the tambourine*]; go, seek a lodging in the city. Gypsies are never safe, they steal and rob whenever they have a chance. Go!

Lydia. I not rob and steal, I make an honest living, Senora. See, see [*shows her a handful of gold. They are astonished.*] I no little thief, no robber — a good Castilian maiden, with lots of love for God and man.

Gertrude. Do you pray?

Lydia. Pray! Surely, Senora, I pray, I sing, I dance, I say my rosary [*shows it*]. I am a good Catholic.

Laurinda. And yet a gypsy!

Lydia. But a good gypsy; let me bring my company in.

Gertrude. How many are in your company?

Lydia. Four, Senora — three and I make four. Oh! surely you will let my companions in [*laughs*]—surely you will.

Gertrude. Well, bring them.   [LYDIA *departs.*]
I hope the Princess will not hear all this noise or find this gypsy tribe here.

Laurinda. I suppose we will have to prepare a nest for them in the room near the iron gate.

Gertrude. Anywhere will do; I surely will not trust them in the house. Here they come!

Enter LYDIA, ROSABELLA, LUCILLA, *disguised;* LYDIA
half dancing and screaming.

Lydia. Here we are Senora. Rosabella, Princess of Valencia.

[ROSABELLA *rushes into* GERTRUDE'S *arms.*]

Rosabella. Oh! kind, sweet Gertrude, thy ninita is here, thy ninita sees. Look at my eyes, Gertrude, I see.

Gertrude. Am I dreaming, or am I Gertrude indeed?

[LUCILLA *goes to* LAURINDA *and the* CHILDREN, *who kiss her hand, laugh and talk in subdued voices.* GERTRUDE *then throws one arm around* AGNES, *whom she kisses.*]

And here is Agnes.

Agnes. Yes, your daughter is here and lives.

Gertrude. Oh, great is God!

Rosabella. And His Holy Mother, who restored my eyes.

Gertrude. Isabella, Isabella! Run to the Princess. Tell Mina that Gertrude desires to see the Princess at once. You must return in a short time; hurry, hurry!

[GERTRUDE *all confused.* ISABELLA *departs in hurry.*]

Rosabella. How is our mother?

Gertrude. She has promised by God to love you; and how can she help it when she sees you now — so lovely, such beautiful eyes. But that gypsy!

Rosabella. Come, Lydia. She was our guide through the mountains.

Lucilla. We sent her ahead to find out if the coast was clear.

Stella. Ha, now I see how she could talk of Rosabella.

[ROSABELLA *and all laugh as* LYDIA *repeats her verses.*]

Lydia. Rosabella — beautiful rose — Lucilla — little light — Rosabella is Lucilla [*bows again and again*].

Gertrude. Oh, how happy I am! Now, how shall

we surprise the Princess? Ha! I know. Go into the room and throw off your cloaks; when I call you, come.

Rosabella. But don't be too long, for I cannot endure it much longer; I must see mamma.

[*Small bell rings. Depart.*

Gertrude. Quick; she is coming — quick! My — what shall I say?

Enter PRINCESS.

Princess. Gertrude, what haste you are in — what made you send to the castle?

Gertrude. Oh, Princess, I cannot tell it! Noble lady, it is too, too good.

Princess. Come, do not be foolish, after you have spoken so wisely. You're full of excitement; what has happened?

Gertrude. Well — well — children — come — come — Rosabella.

All enter. ROSABELLA *and* LUCILLA *rush to their mother, who takes them in her arms.*

Princess. Oh, my children! [*kisses them affectionately*].

Rosabella. Mamma, mamma, see my eyes.

Princess. And you see—you see! What lovely eyes.

Rosabella. It was the dear Virgin in the Grotto of Lourdes. Do you believe now, mamma?

Rosabella and Lucilla [*kneel before the* PRINCESS]. Forgive us, mother, for having left home; but our guardian angels protected us.

Lucilla [*alone*]. And we prayed much, very much for you.

Rosabella. That God may make you happy.

Princess [*folds them in her arms — to the front of the stage*]. Arise, dearest children, it is I who should ask forgiveness, for I have been an unkind mother to you; but the night is over, the day has dawned — my eyes are open, I see my faults. In gratitude we shall all visit Lourdes, and at the shrine of Mary deposit our gifts.

Rosabella. For Mary has cured my bodily blindness and taken away the spiritual blindness from my mother, the noble Princess of Valencia.

CURTAIN.

ACT V

SCENE.—*Grotto, with image of Our Lady.*—ROSA-
BELLA, LUCILLA, PRINCESS *and retinue kneeling before the shrine as curtain rises.—Lights are burning
before the image; flowers and other offerings placed
before it.*

Rosabella. Amen! Now, Senora, we may speak. [*Arise.*] This, then, is heaven's blessed shrine—Mary's abode. See, mother, how fair the Madonna [*points to the statue*]. She looks as lovely as Bernadette described her. Surely, no illiterate, ignorant peasant girl could have portrayed such a vision of unearthly beauty.

Princess. Truly, heaven alone could have inspired it.

Rosabella. Yes, mother; now you believe. [*Takes one hand and leads her to the fount.*] Here I bathed my blind eyes. In this bubbling spring I first saw the image of myself; the happiest moment of my life, when

I was reborn to the world, wandered from darkness to light, and learned to distinguish earth from sky.

Lucilla. Let me send for Bernadette, mother; only then shall our joy be complete.

Princess. Laurinda, dispatch our conveyance to the town.

[LAURINDA *bows, and leaves with* LUCILLA.]

How surprised she will be to find you here, Rosabella.

LUCILLA *quickly enters.*

Lucilla. Bernadette is coming towards the grotto. Dear Bernadette, how happy!

Claps her hands, rushes again from the stage, and returns with BERNADETTE.

Dear little mountain lass, we have kept our promises. Bernadette, here is Rosabella, your friend, the Princess of Valencia!

Bernadette [*astonished and bewildered*]. Princess of Valencia!

Rosabella [*takes both of her hands*]. Yes, dear. Cinderella has changed to a princess; but do not let that worry you, you are so much the more dear to me. Now come, speak to my august mother and mistress. Bernadette — my mother.

Princess [*kisses her forehead*]. Child, you are the cause of my earthly happiness; you have restored my daughter to me, you have brightened my home, and above all you have been instrumental in bringing faith, the true faith, to my heart. How shall I—how can I sufficiently reward you?

Bernadette. Do not speak thus, noble lady. Look upon that beautiful countenance [*points to the image*], the shadow of reality. She, whose image it is, has deigned to appear to me in this cave. Heaven guided your blind daughter to this place, and by Divine power she was cured—I had nothing to do with it. The Queen of Heaven has given the sign, and shown to the world that no mere phantom appeared to me. I rejoice with you, illustrious lady, if a peasant's joy dares to give expression, if it would or could increase your joy.

Princess. You shall no longer remain a peasant. You shall come with us to our ancestral castles, share the earthly honors of my daughters, and teach them by your noble example to serve God and His Holy Mother.

Rosabella and Lucilla. Yes, you must come with us.

Bernadette. It would break my heart to leave my peaceful village, my thatched cottage, my aged mother, and, more than all, this sacred grotto. Your promises are generous and tempting, but that I should accept them — never!

Rosabella [*affectionately*]. Sister — let us call you by that name — sister, pray do not refuse my good mother's offer; come with us.

Bernadette. I would do wrong in accepting. I was born a humble peasant, reared in the heart of the Pyrenees; poor I am now, and poor I shall remain; and when I die a little wooden cross shall tell the history of my uneventful life.

Princess. Do not speak so sadly! Your life has not been uneventful. Children upon their mother's knee shall, in ages to come, learn the story of Bernadette,

the Shepherdess of Lourdes; and each building the
piety of the faithful shall raise here will proclaim your
name. You are thrice blessed!

Bernadette. Too much, too much, illustrious lady!
I am unworthy of this praise. I am only a weak instrument in the hands of God. It should mark out for me
the path of virtue and piety, of charity and love divine.

Princess. If you are determined, then, to remain
here, at least let me offer you some little token of my
gratitude; it will help you in your poverty, it will
assist your invalid parents. Bernadette, accept this
trifle [*offers her gold in a silver case*].

Bernadette [*makes the sign of the cross, and runs
like a frightened deer*]. Gold, gold, gold! [*Falls on her
knees before the Princess.*] How can you tempt me,
noble lady! Gold has destroyed young and innocent
hearts; gold has been the ruin of the world. I need no
gold to support my life; my Father, who is in heaven,
feeds the birds of the air and the fishes of the water—
He feeds me, too. Do not tempt a poor girl. I need
no gold.

Princess [*puts her arm about her neck*]. Noble girl,
good girl! You are indeed worthy that Heaven's Queen
should have displayed her diadem of glory before you.
No wonder you despise gold, after beholding the
eternal treasures; yet receive it, not as a gift for yourself, but for this sacred shrine.

Bernadette [*rises*]. Spare me even that. There is a
good lady living in our Province, the Governor's wife;
she witnessed the miracle worked in favor of your
daughter, then in disguise. She avows the cause of

this shrine, and hopes to be instrumental in erecting a chapel as the Virgin Mary commanded.

Princess. Well, be it as you say. But you must receive a gift in remembrance of God's great deed.

Rosabella. Yes, sister, I have brought you this, only a small cross and chain blessed by the Cardinal of Toledo; wear it for the sake of Rosabella, the blind Princess.

Bernadette. How can I refuse you, Senorita; but let it be the only gift the Shepherdess of Lourdes shall accept.

[*Bows, and* ROSABELLA *throws the chain over her head. She kisses the cross.*]

Rosabella. That's a good girl. Now come and see my dear Gertrude, of whom I told you, who first brought me here [*leads her to* GERTRUDE]. Gertrude!

GERTRUDE *comes from among the ladies.*

Gertrude. God bless thee! I feared I might be deprived the privilege of speaking to thee. Thou hast been so good to my Ninita; God bless thee! [*tries to kiss* BERNADETTE'S *hands*].

Bernadette. You have a true motherly heart, Gertrude. You have been a kind mother to the amiable Princess — heaven has rewarded you.

Gertrude. Yes, a thousand times, surely. Oh! how happy everything would be in our beautiful castle if thou wast with Ninita and Princess Lucilla.

Bernadette. No more of this, Gertrude; I have a poor mother whom I cannot leave — and my Heavenly Mother.

Enter MME. MASSAY, MLLE. VERGEZ, MME. DOZONS.
Others withdraw. BERNADETTE *runs towards* MME.
MASSAY.

Bernadette. Good morning, Madame Massay. What
a happy coincidence; the poor blind gypsy has changed
into a Princess — Rosabella of Valencia [*leads her to
the* PRINCESS].
All. Is it possible!
Mme. Massay. Kindly pardon, Princess, my ill
behavior on a former occasion.
Mme. Dozons and Mlle. Vergez. We too must ask
pardon.
Rosabella. You treated me as I deserved, thus you
are certainly excused. I also thank Madame for the
coin she gave the blind gypsy.
Mme. Massay. The Princess has not forgotten it.
And now I extend to the illustrious Senorita the free-
dom of the Province.
Rosabella. Many thanks. It will no doubt include
my mother, the Princess of Valencia, and her retinue.

[PRINCESS *bows.*]

Mme. Massay. Doubly so; for I have heard of the
great and influential house of Valencia through my
husband, the Governor. I rejoice to welcome you
under such happy auspices.
Princess. A pilgrimage of gratitude to our dear
Mother who has cured my child.
Mme. Massay. This miracle had its effect. It is
known throughout France and Spain. Emperor Napoleon has today issued a proclamation permitting the

erection of a basilica on this spot, and the Church authorities confirmed the miracles. Truly Mary has appeared here.

Princess. Receive this gold—40,000 francs—I had destined for Bernadette, but which she refused. Accept it, noble lady, for the erection of the church [*gives it to her*].

Mme. Massay. God will reward your generosity as He rewarded the piety of the humble Shepherdess of Lourdes, and the great faith of the blind Princess. For generations this place shall be a refuge for the sick, the lame, the blind. Thousands will be cured. Pilgrimages without number, and tokens of gratitude and religious fervor shall arrive from every nation of the world.

Bernadette [*going to the front of the stage*]. All generations shall call her blessed who sanctified this place and consecrated it by her presence, who has taught me by what sweet prayer we should venerate her, the "Holy Rosary," and by what title we shall name her when she answered my humble request by saying: "I am the Immaculate Conception."

> [*All turn towards the Grotto, leaving the centre of stage free, and sing the hymn of praise.* VILLAGE CHILDREN *bring flowers, others take water from the fountain. All group themselves gracefully on the stage, which is gorgeously illuminated.*]

CURTAIN.

FINIS.

www.ingramcontent.com/pod-product-compliance
Lightning Source LLC
Chambersburg PA
CBHW031248260626
47169CB00007B/2497